Dear Parents:

Congratulations! Your child is taking the first steps on an exciting journey. The destination? Independent reading!

STEP INTO READING® will help your child get there. The program offers five steps to reading success. Each step includes fun stories and colorful art or photographs. In addition to original fiction and books with favorite characters, there are Step into Reading Non-Fiction Readers, Phonics Readers and Boxed Sets, Sticker Readers, and Comic Readers—a complete literacy program with something to interest every child.

Learning to Read, Step by Step!

Ready to Read   Preschool–Kindergarten
• big type and easy words • rhyme and rhythm • picture clues
For children who know the alphabet and are eager to begin reading.

Reading with Help   Preschool–Grade 1
• basic vocabulary • short sentences • simple stories
For children who recognize familiar words and sound out new words with help.

Reading on Your Own   Grades 1–3
• engaging characters • easy-to-follow plots • popular topics
For children who are ready to read on their own.

Reading Paragraphs   Grades 2–3
• challenging vocabulary • short paragraphs • exciting stories
For newly independent readers who read simple sentences with confidence.

Ready for Chapters   Grades 2–4
• chapters • longer paragraphs • full-color art
For children who want to take the plunge into chapter books but still like colorful pictures.

STEP INTO READING® is designed to give every child a successful reading experience. The grade levels are only guides; children will progress through the steps at their own speed, developing confidence in their reading.

Remember, a lifetime love of reading starts with a single step!

© 2014 Viacom International Inc. and Viacom Overseas Holdings C.V. All rights reserved.
Published in the United States by Random House Children's Books, a division of Random House
LLC, 1745 Broadway, New York, NY 10019, and in Canada by Random House of Canada Limited,
Toronto, Penguin Random House Companies. Nickelodeon, Teenage Mutant Ninja Turtles, and
all related titles, logos, and characters are trademarks of Viacom International Inc. and Viacom
Overseas Holdings C.V. Based on characters created by Peter Laird and Kevin Eastman.

Step into Reading, Random House, and the Random House colophon are registered trademarks of
Random House LLC.

Visit us on the Web!
StepIntoReading.com
randomhouse.com/kids

Educators and librarians, for a variety of teaching tools, visit us at RHTeachersLibrarians.com

ISBN 978-0-385-38506-0 (trade) — ISBN 978-0-385-38507-7 (lib. bdg.)

Printed in the United States of America

10

nickelodeon

TEENAGE MUTANT NINJA TURTLES™

PIZZA PARTY!

Based on the screenplay "Day One, Part One"
by Joshua Sternin and Jeffrey Ventimilia

Illustrated by Patrick Spaziante

Random House 🏠 New York

Four mutant turtles live
in the sewers
of New York City.

They are brothers.

They are ninjas.

Leo is the leader.

Raph likes to fight.

Donnie can build
anything.
Mikey is a joker.

The Turtles leave
the sewers
for the first time.

New York City is
dark and dirty.
The Turtles love it!

The man is afraid
of the giant turtles.
He drops a box.

What is in the box?

It is pizza!

"Pizza is the best!"

says Mikey.

The Turtles hear
a scream.

Two men in blue
are grabbing
a girl!

Leo leads the attack!

Raph jumps into action!

Donnie swings his staff.

Pow!
The man falls
to the ground.

Mikey discovers that the men are really robots!

Small pink aliens are inside the robots! They are called the Kraang.

The Kraang escape!

The Turtles save the girl.

Her name is April O'Neil.

"I know how
we can celebrate,"
Mikey says.

Pizza party!

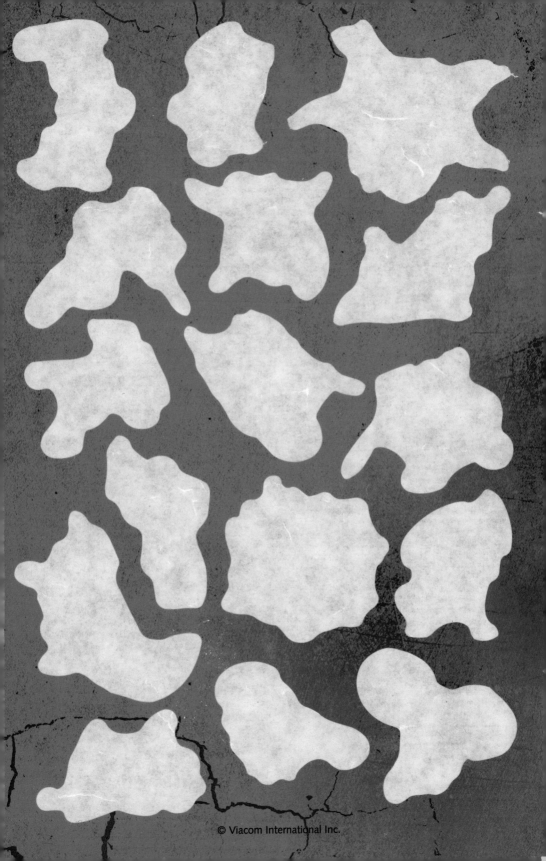

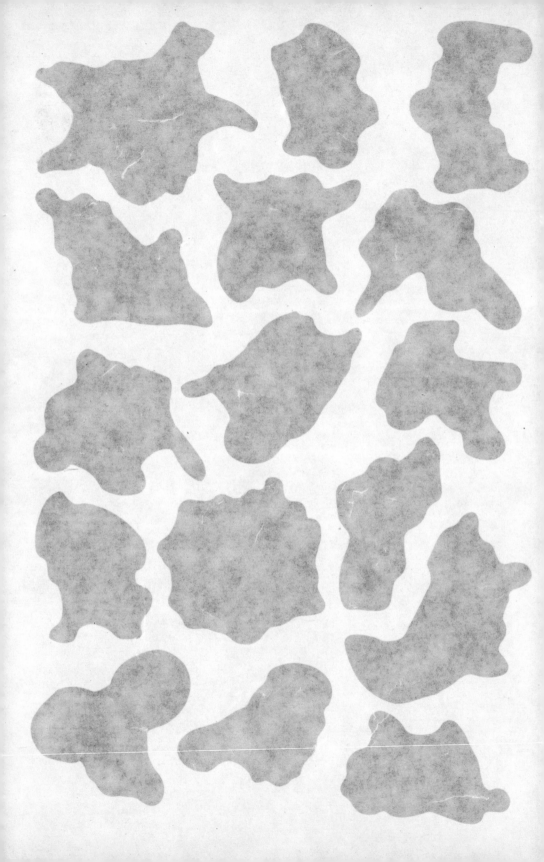